MICHAEL
WHO MISSED HIS TRAIN

by

Dorothy and Marguerite Bryan

Junior Books

DOUBLEDAY, DORAN & COMPANY, INC.

NEW YORK

1941

a
2/c
22c
6c
D

MICHAEL
WHO MISSED HIS TRAIN

ONE morning the expressman delivered a large box to the mother of Mary and David. The children wondered what was in it.

It humped! It heaved! It sniffed!

A shiny eye peered out between the slats that were nailed across the side. Then there was a bark!

"It's a dog!" shouted Mary and David.

"Yes, it's Michael from Boston," said their mother. "But we already have Patsy, and we really cannot keep more than one dog on this small place, so Michael will have to go back to Boston as soon as he has had a little rest."

When Michael was taken out of the box, he proved to be a very friendly Sealyham terrier with big feet, big brown eyes, and a fine, strong tail for wagging.

He did not have the big brown spot over his right eye that Patsy had but he had small spots on his ears.

Mary and David and Patsy decided that they did not want Michael to go back to Boston. So they all met out under the dogwood tree to plan what to do about it.

"Mother loves Patsy and wants *her* to stay," David said. "Do you suppose it is because Patsy does tricks?"

They all turned and looked at Patricia.
She sat up and waved her paws.
"Patsy sits up," said Mary. "Why don't you sit up, Michael?"

Michael tried very hard, but when he had lifted his big front paws off the ground he leaned way toward one side,

then way toward the other side,

then w-a-y, W-A-Y back,

and over he rolled!

But Michael tried again and again until he could sit up, too— though he did not look very steady.

They all ran indoors to Mother. "Sit up," Mary ordered.

Patsy sat up very straight, lightly waving her paws.

Michael tried once and fell over; tried twice and fell over; tried the third time, and sat up! His chest stuck way out; his paws dangled way down; he wobbled and he tottered—but he did *not* tumble over.

"That is very smart," admired Mother. "But one beggar is bad enough around this house. What would we do with two? Michael must go back to Boston."

What to do? Michael was so willing—so loving—so anxious to make himself wanted.

Michael chased balls and sticks.

But he chased the cat next door, and *that* did not help!

Michael stretched himself tenderly on Mother's feet whenever she sat down.

But he stretched himself tenderly on the best silk cushion when he was lonesome for Mother's feet and THAT did not help!

When Patsy was eating her dinner, Michael just
sat and watched politely, and no matter how s-l-o-w-l-y Patsy mincey-
moused her dinner he would not steal a crumb.

But he brought home a large soup bone that belonged to some-
body else and THAT did not help!

Michael taught himself to sing softly—woo!   woo!! WOO!!!
But he taught Patsy to sing, too, and whenever those two were left
alone on the front seat of the automobile they
w-o-o-! W-O-O!! W-O-O-ED!!!
together, louder and louder until everybody came running to see what
the trouble was.
And that CERTAINLY did not help!

Whenever Michael did anything wrong, he put himself in the corner behind the door and tried not to do it again.

But somehow he was apt to forget to be a good dog, and THAT DID NOT HELP AT ALL!

So Mother said, "Michael means well, but he *must* go back to Boston."

Mary, David, Patsy, and Michael all met out under the weeping-
willow tree. Patsy sat close beside Mary and kissed the tip of Michael's
nose. "What shall we try now?" asked David.

"We will have to try a brand new surprise trick," answered Mary. "We must all put on our thinking caps."

So Mary made them each a newspaper hat, and they sat thinking — and *thinking* — and THINKING — and **THINKING**.

Then strange sounds began to come out from under the weeping-willow tree — whistlings and tootlings and thumpings and excited yippings. And a whole barrel of ginger snaps was used up as rewarding tid-bits.

After a long, long time Mary, David, Patsy, and Michael went tramping in to Mother.

David kept whistling the first few bars of "Yankee Doodle," over and over.

They all came to a stop in front of Mother's chair.

Patsy and Michael listened carefully. Everything was very quiet. Then— "TA-RA-RA-RA-RA-RA

BOOM!" said David.

At the word "Boom!" Patsy and Michael fell on their sides and lay just as still as still.

"DI-YAY!" cried Mary.

Patsy and Michael jumped to their feet as though they had been pulled by one string.

"They died for their country," explained David.

"And came alive again for you," added Mary.

"That is very clever," applauded Mother. "But Michael must REALLY GO BACK TO BOSTON!!"

Mournful Michael!

So Michael was put into his box again and the slats were nailed across the side.

Mary and David counted out enough dog biscuits to last during the whole trip to Boston.

Crunch! Scrunch! Munch-munch!! went Michael—and all his meals for his trip to Boston were eaten up before he had even started. Michael was very loving and very sad at leaving—but, somehow, he was *always* hungry.

When the last biscuit crumb was licked up all was still.

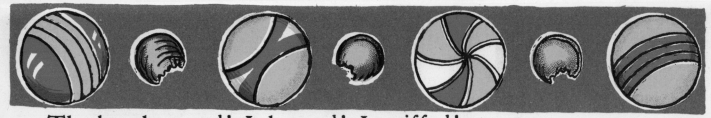

The box humped! It heaved! It sniffed!

A sorrowful eye peered out between the slats nailed across the side.

Then there was a moan!

"I will get out the car and take Michael to his train," Mother said hastily.

"Oh, please! Won't you let us carry him down ourselves?" begged Mary. "He isn't heavy."

"And it isn't far," added David.

"Well, all right," said Mother. "Be careful. Good-bye, Michael. I am sorry to see you leave, but we really cannot keep more than one dog on this small place, so you must go back to Boston." She patted Michael's nose through the slats and went quickly into the house.

Mary carried one end of Michael's box, and David held the other end. Patsy followed.

Slowly, slowly they walked along.

"Let's give him some soft leaves for a bed on his way to Boston," Mary suggested.

So they put down the box and gathered oak leaves and pushed them between the slats.

Michael scratched round and round and made himself a cosy nest. Slowly, slowly they moved on.

"He likes to toss pine cones," David said. "Let's find a nice big one for Michael to play with on his way to Boston."

So they put down the box and Patsy found a big pine cone that they squeezed in between the slats.

Michael nosed it and nibbled it but he could not toss it very well. There was not enough room. So he buried it under the oak leaves.

Slowly, slowly they trudged on.

"Do you want to change hands?" Mary asked. "My right arm is getting tired."

"All right," answered David. "So is my left arm."

So they put down the box and changed sides. They both patted Michael between the bars on the way around the box.

Slowly, slowly they tramped on.

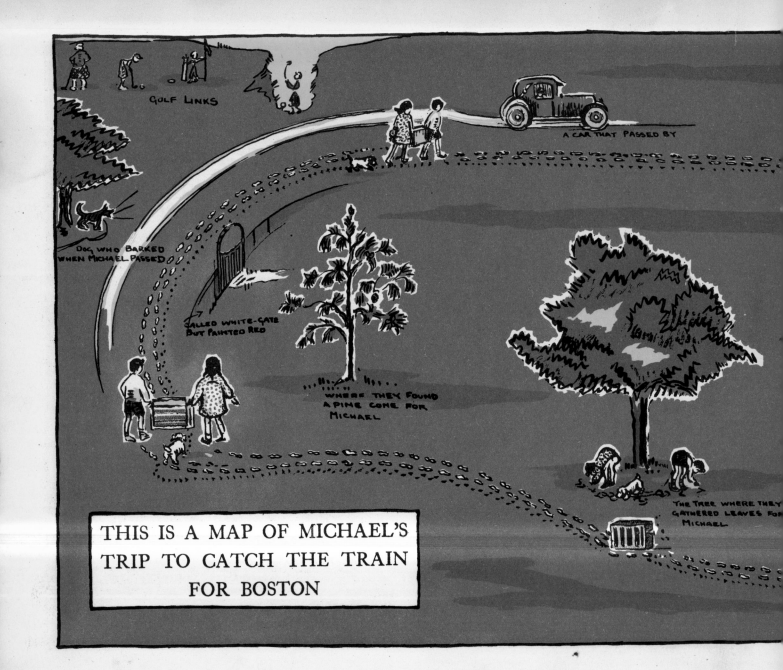

Mary and David had just changed hands again when—
TOOT! TOOT!
"It's the train!" cried Mary.
"And we haven't Michael's ticket or anything," shouted David.
They started to run.

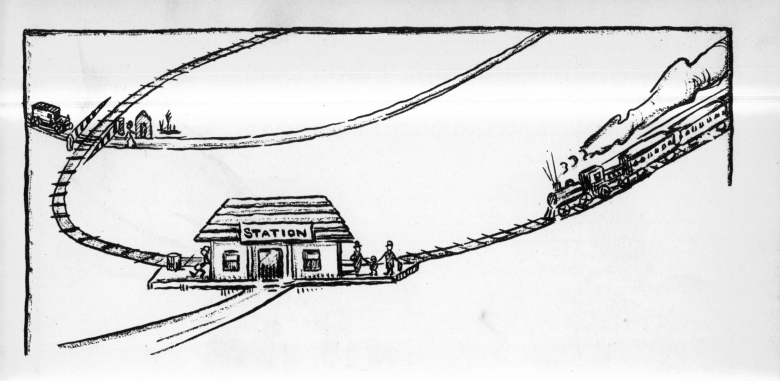

The box kept bumping their legs.
Michael rolled from side to side, barking and scratching.
Patsy ran, too.
Just as they rushed around the last curve in the path,
TOOT! TOOT—TOOT!!
the train gave a warning whistle and PUFF—*puff—puff*, it pulled out
of the station.

They put down the box.
"MICHAEL HAS MISSED HIS TRAIN!" cried David.
"So he has," said Mary.

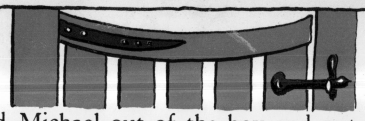

Mary and David pulled Michael out of the box and put him down beside Patsy. Slowly, slowly they trudged back to Mother, who was waiting at home, feeling rather lonely.

"Michael has missed his train," cried Mary and David.
There was a pause. They waited anxiously.
"What! Michael has missed his train," said Mother. "Well, then,
of course—

"Michael *cannot* go back to Boston."